BOTTOM'S UP

SHARON KIZZIAH-HOLMES

Paperback-Press
an imprint of A & S Publishing
A & S Holmes, Inc.

ISBN-13: 978-1-945669-19-4

DEDICATION

Shelly and Chris, Aunt Sharon loves you. =)

ACKNOWLEDGEMENTS

Thanks to my BFF Norma for her wonderful editing skills, and for giving me the perfect name for this story.

To my husband, I know I've said this before but, thank you for your support in everything I do.

Last but not least, Shelly, my favorite middle niece. Thank you for your patience in waiting an extra year for your Christmas gift. I hope you enjoy reading *Bottom's Up* as much as I did writing it.

Love to my family.

.

CHAPTER 1

Chris Wayne lay on his side on the examining table of the Urgent Care unit at a Las Vegas clinic. How the hell could this kind of freak accident happen? A piece of glass, from a broken stage light stuck in the cheek of his backside was the last thing he needed during his week-long gig at Caesars Palace.

He was thankful his best friend and lead guitar player, Dennis Aaron was setting up his equipment when this happened. Otherwise, he would have had to drive himself to the clinic. Sitting sideways on one cheek wouldn't have been the safest way to get there. Right now it wasn't a laughing matter, but he was sure in the future his injury would be the butt of many jokes.

Laughing at his own thoughts, he heard a knock

at the door. A beautiful nurse walked in carrying a chart. Her dark hair was the perfect contrast to bring out the beauty of her big blue eyes. Damn, she was gorgeous!

"Mr…," she glanced at the chart.

"Wayne. Chris Wayne." He had given his real name to the front desk hoping to stay incognito. He got tired of all the hoopla associated with being a country music star. If he'd told them Chris Brock, his stage name, it would have been public knowledge he was there.

She put the chart down, met his gaze and offered him a handshake. "Mr. Wayne, I'm NP Shelly Jinsen. I'll be taking care of you today."

God he hoped she didn't recognize him. His butt cheek was killing him. All he wanted was for the doctor to come, get the glass out and sew him up. Her hand was small and soft yet her grip was firm when he grasped it. "Nice to meet you, ma'am. So, you're gonna take more info. then the doc'll come in?"

"My assistant already got all the information we need. I'm here to treat what ails you."

He was so confused. "So you're the doctor?" She was a pretty one, if she was.

"No, I'm the NP on duty. As I said, I'll be the one to take care of all of your needs today."

"What the hell is an NP?" If she thought he was going to…well, just out and out turn his rear end up to her for a close up look, she had another think coming.

"There's no need for profanity, sir."

Was that a spark of anger in her eyes? She was

right, he shouldn't have talked to her that way, but his situation would have been embarrassing enough had she been a man. "I apologize, ma'am, but I'm a little stressed right now."

A smile lifted the corners of her mouth. "From what I see on the chart, you have reason to be. How did you get a piece of glass stuck in the cheek of your backside?" She stood up and started toward him. "Let me take a look."

He held his hand up to stop her from getting any closer. "Ma'am, please, just send a man doctor in here and everything will be okay." He didn't know what an NP was, but he knew a nurse couldn't do what he needed done.

She stopped in her tracks. "Mr. Wayne, I'm a licensed Nurse Practitioner. I take care of patients in this clinic all day long, five days a week. I can, and do, perform most tasks the doctors around here do."

"No disrespect, ma'am, but I'd rather see a doctor. A man doctor. I mean, I'm sure you're good at what you do, but…well–."

"Mr. Wayne." This time she held up her hand to shush him. "I'll make you a deal." She reached into a drawer and pulled out a hospital gown. "You put this on, and I'll see what I can do to find a male NP to take care of you."

"Aren't there any doctors here? What kind of urgent care place is this?" Oooh, that ruffled her feathers, but he had his pride to keep.

"Nurse Practitioners are highly trained medical professionals. I assure you, everything will be fine. That is, *if* I can find a man to get that piece of glass out of your a–rear!" She put the gown down on one of the chairs in the small room. "Put that on." Then she turned and started toward the door.

"But–."

She grabbed the door knob, however, she didn't open the door. "But what?"

"Well, I can't put that on." He heard her take a deep breath then let it out. He was really getting under her skin, and he kind of enjoyed it.

"Why not, Mr. Wayne?"

"Um, 'cause there's kind of a little problem with getting my jeans down over that piece of glass in my a–rear." Heat rushed up his neck and he knew he was totally red faced. The snicker that escaped her pretty little mouth didn't help anything, either.

Letting go of the knob, she faced him once again. "I'm sorry, I didn't mean to laugh. I'll send my nurse in to cut them off. She'll be here in a minute to get you prepped. You know, the longer you put off getting treated, the better chance you have of getting an infection in your wound."

She was telling the truth, and he didn't know why he was so embarrassed. It wasn't like other women hadn't seen his bare butt. Although, it had been a while. He didn't make it a habit of sleeping with 'groupies' like other guys in the business did. Relationships meant something more to him than a one night stand.

He looked at the woman standing in front of him. Her medical coat was unbuttoned and hung freely to each side of her business-type suit. It revealed a perfectly shaped body to go with her perfectly shaped, kissable lips.

She looked like someone he could have a

relationship with. What? What was he thinking? *Get that thought out of your head right now, Wayne. A woman is the last thing you need! Much less one you're fixing to let pull a piece of glass out of your butt and sew up the cut.*

Still on his side, he propped himself up with his elbow and rested his head on his hand then met her gaze. He was defeated. "Okay, you win. Get these jeans cut off of me and do your thing."

"I'm glad you had a moment of sanity." Why did this man look so familiar? Had she gone to school with him or something? Oh, well, she couldn't think about that now, it had been a long day; she was tired she wanted to go home.

"Thanks, Doc. I mean, Nurse."

The way that crooked smile of his almost made her not want to slap him for being...what...quite handsome...vulnerable, at that moment...and probably a liar like most men she knew besides her father? "Mr. Wayne–."

"Please, if we're going to be intimate, call me Chris."

"Intimate?"

"You are going to be caressing my buttocks aren't you?"

How did he make her smile so easily when she was this tired? She wasn't going to answer that, though she liked his sense of humor. "Okay, Chris. You relax. I'll be right back." The door knob was cool to the touch, but her hand was still warm from the man's handshake.

She was glad to be in the hallway. Standing in the small room with that handsome devil made her more than a little shaky. She'd never had that kind of reaction to a man. He made her feel like she did when she was cheerleader in Denver City, TX on her first date with the high school quarterback, and he wasn't even that cute!

Willing her legs to move, she approached the nurse's station. "Sidne, we're going to have to cut the jeans off of that guy in exam room 5. Would you cart up everything we need to do that, and to suture him up, please?"

The nurse smiled and nodded her head. "Yes, ma'am. He's pretty good looking. I can't wait to see what's under those tight fitting Wranglers."

A sudden surge of jealousy coursed through her…but why? She had no reason to feel that way. "Cool off, missy, we have a job to do." She liked Sid a lot and was glad she was her assistant.

"Oh, all right, you party pooper. You need to stop being so serious and have a little fun. Your biological clock isn't getting any younger, you know."

Raising one eyebrow, she gave the younger woman a warning glance. "I have plenty of fun, and I'm not getting old." Heck, she was only twenty nine. She had plenty of time on her 'biological clock'.

"When you're ready to prep Mr. Faded Wranglers, let me know. We'll call one of the male aids in to observe. Don't want any sexual harassment claims made on us." She always liked to hear Sid laugh, it was contagious and she needed a good laugh after this day.

Shelly heard the prep cart being wheeled up the hallway. It was time to face the man again, but this time she wouldn't be looking into his eyes. Smiling at the thought, she turned toward her assistant. "Ready, Sid?"

"Let's go get those jeans off that hunk."

The young woman was incorrigible. "Tell you what, I'll take the cart in the room and start getting ready while you go get Josh." She knew Sidne had a crush on Josh and if he was in the room, she'd be less likely to make remarks that might embarrass Chris more than he already was. Although, it was kind of fun to watch his face turn red, but her job was to make him feel at ease with his care, not to cause him distress.

Taking the cart, she began to roll it down the hallway. When she stopped in front of exam room 5, her heart started to race. Why was she so nervous?

She inhaled a calming breath, let it out then knocked on the door. Chris' deep voice resonated from the other side.

"Come in."

She turned the knob then entered the room, rolling the cart in front of her. Her breath caught in her throat when she realized he'd taken off his shirt. His tanned, bare, very smooth muscular chest made her primal instincts go wild. *You have **got** to get a grip! He's a patient, not a man.*

That was the dumbest thing she'd ever thought, but at least it might help her get through this procedure without swooning. "It's good to see you're halfway ready." She forced a confident smile, although she didn't feel confident at all.

"Thanks, I figured I may as well get started being naked."

"Well, don't worry, you won't be totally naked. You get to wear this." She picked up the hospital gown. "Remember?"

"Oh, yes, I'm gonna look real cute."

"You'd better take off your belt. We don't want to cut through that. I'll help you get your cowboy boots off, too."

He started to laugh. "That would look cute now wouldn't it? Me running around in a silly looking gown wearing my boots." He handed her his belt. "Hmm, if you cut my pants off, then what am I going to wear when I leave."

She took the leather belt and noticed the beautiful western buckle. It was silver with the gold letters CB imbedded in it. If his name was Chris Wayne, why would his buckle say CB? That didn't matter. What did matter was getting that glass removed and heading him out of here so she could get her hormones under control.

"Well, I guess you'll just have to keep the gown for your very own." His smile not only lit up the room, but warmed her heart.

"Ain't gonna happen, ma'am. My friend Dennis is in the waiting room. If you don't mind, would you have someone ask him to go and get me some more jeans?"

"I'll see what I can do, but right now, let's get those boots off."

Chris could tell the woman hadn't pulled off to many pairs of cowboy boots, if any, but she sure looked pretty trying. "Ouch!"

"Oh, my gosh! Did I hurt your foot?"

Her eyes were riddled with concern, but he couldn't let her worry. "No, just got crossways with the glass a little. I'm okay."

Someone knocked at the door. He watched Nurse Shelly straighten, smooth her hair and try to put herself back together after playing tug of war with his boot. Her voice wasn't at all pleasant when she spoke. Was she irritated that she couldn't defeat his footwear?

"Come in."

A man and a woman, both dressed in scrubs, entered the room. He swallowed the lump in his throat. It was time to get this party started, and all he could do was focus on the beautiful nurse practitioner.

"Mr. Wayne, this is my assistant, Sidne, and nurses aid Josh."

"Howdy y'all." He met the nurses aid's gaze. "Josh, think you can help me out of my boots? The lady here can't seem to get it done." Shelly shot him a disapproving glance which he just smiled at while the young man heaved the boots off his feet.

"Put this on with the opening in the back."

"Yes, ma'am, you're the boss." He donned the sloppy garment then watched Shelly and her assistant put on gloves. The younger woman tore open a package of funny looking scissors and handed them to Shelly.

"Okay, Chris, are you ready?"

He liked the way she said his name. "I'm ready."

"Would you turn onto your stomach for me?"

Once he was on his belly and settled, he felt the cool edge of the instrument against his skin and heard the first snip. It only took a couple of minutes for her to cut the denim pants completely off, then she clipped off his boxer briefs. A cool breeze wafted across his backside.

"Well, there it is." Shelly put the scissors on the cart.

"My butt?"

"No, Mr. Wayne, the glass is fully exposed."

"And my butt's not?" He heard a slight giggle, but knew it wasn't Shelly, so it had to be her assistant.

"You are a funny guy. Sid, hand me the iodine. I want to sterilize the area."

The wet cloth touched his skin. "That's cold."

"It's better to be safe then to risk infection."

She had a gentle touch and he wondered what her bare hand would feel like rubbing his derriere in a different situation. How could he be having sexual thoughts when she was about to stick a needle in him?

"You're lucky this isn't a bigger shard. You would be in a mess. Once we get it out, you should only have to have five or six stitches."

"Awesome." She took the cloth away and immediately he missed her touching him.

"Sid, give me the Lidocaine syringe, please?" She paused. "Thank you. Now, Chris, I'm going to deaden this before I pull the glass out. It's going to sting a little."

Boy, she wasn't kidding. "Damn, woman." The sting went deeper and he realized he shouldn't tick her off in the middle of this. He fought to keep his breath steady. "Sorry. I know you're only doing your job."

Chris Wayne had one of the nicest tushes she'd ever seen. "Try to be still. This part's done and it will only be a minute before I pull the glass out."

She placed one flap of the gown over his butt and waited for the medicine to kick in. It was one thing to work on him like this, but if she left that backside exposed, she feared all she'd do was stare at it's nice, round shape.

The small talk Josh and Sidne made was a welcome break to the silence. She was thankful for their presence in the room. It made things less awkward. She moved the gown out of the way and gave the injured area a slight pinch with the tweezer tool. "Chris, can you feel that?"

"I guess not."

"Sid, hand me the large tweezer scissors and let's get this puppy out of there."

"Here you go."

Taking the tool with her right hand, she placed her left hand around the glass sticking out of his skin. His rear was firm and perfectly shaped. Too bad it would have this little scar on it. However, she guessed it could give him…character, in a way.

"Better get plenty of gauze, because once I pull this out, it's really going to bleed." She glanced up at Josh. "Hey, if you don't mind, would you go to the lobby and find...what's your friend's name, Mr. Wayne?"

"Dennis Aaron."

"Mr. Aaron, and ask him to bring Mr. Wayne a pair of sweats to go home in?"

"Sweats? I don't own a pair of sweats."

"I don't think you're going to want to wear a pair of tight jeans for a few days. Maybe he can go to the local box store and pick some up. Or, like I told you, you are welcome to wear the gown home."

CHAPTER 2

Chris pulled on the sweat pants the D-man had brought him then donned the new tennis shoes. He was so used to wearing cowboy boots he felt out of place, but thankfully it was only temporary.

He waited for Nurse Shelly to come back to give him his paperwork. Today was the first time in a long time he had met a woman that tripped his trigger. He really wanted to get acquainted with her, but his week in Vegas was gone and only the weekend was left. That threw a wrench into that.

If he didn't have a show Saturday night and matinee on Sunday, at least he could spend more time with her. Sometimes having hit records and being on the road so many days a year, wasn't all it was cracked up to be.

Most people thought it was a glamorous life, but they didn't have to live on a bus, be in a different town every night, sleep in a strange bed a lot of the time and most of all, be lonely. Sure, the guys were his friends, but it wasn't the same as having that special someone by your side. Or even knowing they would be waiting for you the next time you got home.

Damn, Shelly created a definite wave of emotion in him. Maybe he'd offer her a ticket to the show. No, he would like for her to know him as Chris Wayne before she found out he was Chris Brock. A light wrap sounded at the door then he heard Shelly's voice.

"You decent?"

"Depends on what you mean by that. If you mean am I dressed, yes." He saw the smile on her face when she walked in. She was so pretty and he liked the fact that he could make her laugh.

She handed him a plastic bag. "Here is something you can take your clothes home in, although your jeans and underwear are pretty much ruined since we cut them off of you. I doubt you'll want to keep them."

"Thanks." He took her hand when she gave the bag to him. He met the gaze of those mesmerizing blue eyes. She was one hell of a beautiful woman. "I really mean it. Thank you for stitching me up."

Electricity shot through Shelly's hand, up her arm and straight to her heart. How did he affect her this way? His eyes sparkled with genuine kindness and gratefulness. They were blue like hers and she felt comforted by them. "You're welcome. Just doing my job."

If he only knew how she'd had to steady her hand before sewing him up, he may not be so grateful. He was someone she thought she could let into her life. That is, if she wasn't going to move to San Angelo in a month. She refused to have a long distance relationship. Chris living in Las Vegas just wouldn't work. Her residency was over and she longed to be with her family again.

Why was she even thinking of that? He was a stranger, for goodness sake. A stranger she was attracted to? Absolutely, but that's it. End of story.

"Yeah, well." He chuckled. "You had to go above and beyond today. I mean, to have to look at my butt was kind of up close and personal."

It was hard for her not to laugh, however, she couldn't help but grin. Funny how he made her do that often. "I've seen a lot of backsides over the last few years and yours is quite nice." What? Had she really just said that? "I mean…well…I-I mean–" His laughter filled the room and she was glad all the other patients of the day had left or everyone on the floor would have heard it reverberate through the walls. How could she stop herself from laughing? He knew that moment had been awkward for her and he'd made it not so embarrassing by his laughter.

"Thank you for the compliment…I think."

The moment he got serious and he stepped toward her she found it hard to breathe. Was he going to try to kiss her? She hoped not, yet she hoped so. Damn she was so confused.

"Shelly?" He took her by the shoulders. "How about having lunch with me tomorrow."

She met his gaze. "Lunch?"

"Yes, the meal most people eat in the middle of the day?" he said with a smile.

She had Friday afternoons off. It would be perfect, but she dare not. Before her brain engaged, her heart propelled her answer forward. "Okay."

"Great!" He stepped back. "How about the Mesa Grill at Caesars?"

Mesa Grill. That was a pretty high-toned place and she loved their corn tamale with shrimp dish. She swallowed the lump in her throat. "One o'clock okay?"

He nodded and picked up his bag of clothes. "I'll be there with bells on."

A picture of him wearing only bells around his…no, she couldn't let her thoughts go there. "You'd better wear loose pants for the next few days. You don't want to break your stitches open."

"I'll see you tomorrow at one."

That sexy smile and his tone told her he probably was going to wear whatever he wanted. "I'm warning you, Mr. Wayne, don't put tight jeans on for the next few days. You might regret it."

"Thanks for the warning, Doc. I mean, Nurse."

When he shut the door behind him, she sat on the side of the exam table, took a deep breath and tried to slow her racing pulse. Had she really accepted a lunch date with a stranger? What was she thinking?

~~~

"Hey, Shel, want to go to the Brock show Saturday night at Caesars? I've got an extra ticket."

Shelly finished shutting down her office computer. In less than an hour, she'd be meeting Chris Wayne for lunch! Butterflies did a happy dance in her stomach. She couldn't stop thinking about the man.

"Shel?"

Grabbing her purse out of the desk drawer, Shelly glanced up at Sidne. "Oh, sorry. I was thinking about something else."

"Could it be that handsome cowboy that was in here yesterday? I noticed the way you two were looking at each other."

"Oh, stop."

"No, really, I'm surprised he didn't ask you out."

She couldn't keep it to herself any longer, she was too excited. "Well…"

Sidne giggled like a school girl then rushed to hug Shelly. "He did, didn't he?"

Now she was giggling like a teenager. "Yes! I'm going to meet him now for lunch…at the Mesa Grill."

"Ooooh, pretty hoity toity for a cowboy. He must think you're really special."

One thing was for sure, she thought Chris was special. It had been a long time since she'd been interested in getting to know a man better, and for the life of her, she didn't know why it was him. A cowboy? Really? "I know, right?"

"Call me and let me know how it goes."

Shelly glanced at her watch. "I'd better get

going. Hope I'm not late."

"Hey, being fashionably late is…well…fashionable."

"Sid, you're crazy!" She hugged the other girl. "I'll see you Monday." She started to walk away, but stopped when she heard her friend's voice.

"Wait, you didn't answer my question."

"What's that?"

"Do you want to go to the Brock concert tomorrow night?"

Where had she heard that name before? "Brock? Who's that?"

"He's a country singer that's trending right now. His latest song is a remake of a hit song from the 1970's. It was by a guy named Tommy Overstreet."

"Oh, I've heard of Tommy Overstreet. My dad used to play his stuff when I was a kid. I've just never gotten into country music much, so…I don't know."

"Brock's hit on the radio right now is Heaven is My Woman's Love. The seats are front row. Can't get any better than that."

She had to get out of there; she was surely going to be late for lunch now. "Like I said, I'm not that big on country."

"You need to get a life. One country concert isn't going to kill you. You may enjoy it, who knows."

What did she have to lose? "Why not. Eat at Caesars today; go to a show there tomorrow." She walked through the doorway and down the hall. "I'll call you later." She heard Sidne's voice request after her.

"Hey, wish I had another ticket. You could ask

the cowboy to go."

The last thing she would do was ask a man out on a date, no matter how much she liked him. She gave a dismissive wave to the other woman and left the building, hoping she didn't get into a lot of lunch time traffic on her way to Caesars.

~~~~

Chris waited outside the door of the Mesa Grill. He couldn't understand why he was so jittery about having lunch with Ms. Shelly Jinsen. There had been little time, since he'd left her office yesterday, he hadn't thought about her. Even through the rough sound check for the show that morning, the band and crew could tell he was distracted.

For the tenth time in the last five minutes he glanced at his watch. She was late. Was she going to stand him up? His heart sank. What if she'd been in an accident?

Tell her who you are! He wanted to tell her who he was, but he feared she would either be star eyed, like most women he met, or she'd run the other way. Neither of those options is what he wanted. No, this woman wasn't shallow; she was intelligent and gorgeous. Surely she'd accept his identity with grace and cha–.

There she was, walking toward him, even more beautiful than he remembered, and sexy as hell. A tidal wave of relief pulsed through him that she didn't stand him up. How could he have doubted she would keep her word? He knew better.

The curves of her body and the sway of her hips

as she approached made his blood run hot. She was magnificent. He wondered how her curves and bare skin would feel in his arms, how those kissable lips would taste, how she'd say his name in the heat of passion. Okay, this was ridiculous. He almost felt like he was falling in love with this awesome creature and he didn't even know her. Falling in love was one thing, but love at first sight? Wild.

"Hi, sorry I'm late. Didn't get out of the office on time." Shelly's heart was beating a million miles an hour and those damn butterflies in her stomach just wouldn't be still. How did just seeing this man do that to her?

"Hey, no worries. I've only been here a few minutes. You ready to eat?"

Shelly hoped her throat would allow her to swallow, as nervous as she was. "I'm starving."

"Good."

He turned and offered his arm to escort her inside. "Oh, you're a gentleman I see."

"Born and raised a Texan. I was taught to treat a lady right."

"Texas?" She wondered how he'd treat a lady in the bedroom. He had a nice muscular chest and backside. She would only imagine what other things were like. *Shelly, get that stuff out of your head. You don't even know this guy!*

"Yes, ma'am."

They followed the greeter to a table where Chris pulled out her chair and helped her get seated. She watched him gracefully walk to the other side and carefully sit down. "What part of Texas?"

"Abilene. I've lived there all my life."

Abilene? That was less than a hundred miles from San Angelo. "What made you to move to Vegas?"

He laughed and shook his head. "I don't live here. I'm just passing through. I have a ranch about thirty miles south of Abilene on 277. There's no way I'd ever live anywhere but my home state."

Her heart threatened to stop! This was incredible. His ranch was less than an hour away from where she was moving? "You're kidding!"

"No, ma'am. I'm a bonafide Texan through and through. Just like my friend the D-man. We're brothers from another mother. Why would you think I'm kidding you?"

Should she tell him? What if he wanted to see her after she moved to San Angelo? Was she ready for that? He was the first man to make her feel such emotion after just meeting. Maybe God put them in each other's path. *Lord, please lead me to do the right thing.* "It's not that I thought you were really kidding me, it's just that...I-I..."

"Spit it out, girl. Just that what?"

She met his azure gaze and her heart compelled her to speak. "I'm moving to San Angelo next month. I have a job at the Shannon Clinic."

The waiter stepped up to the table. "May I take your order?"

Chris looked at the menu, but couldn't see the words. His mind was in a whirl. She was moving to

San Angelo. She'd be so close. Was this what *fate* meant? Were they supposed to be together? Had he just met his soul mate? Questions flew through his head. When Shelly gave her order, her voice pulled him back to reality.

"I'll have the corn tamale with shrimp, and a glass of Pinot Grigio, please." She closed her menu and handed it to the server.

"Wonderful choice, ma'am." The waiter turned toward Chris. "And what will it be for you, sir?"

"Ah…oh…ah…I guess I'll have the same thing except skip the wine and bring me a lite beer."

"Yes, sir, coming right up."

Sitting back in his chair, Chris fumbled with his silverware and tried to act like he wasn't fazed by the news, when in reality, he was thrilled. "Really? Why, you'll only be a hop, skip and a jump from me."

"I know. How coincidental, right?"

No matter how coincidental their meeting was, he thought maybe it was supposed to be. "Right. Hey, possibly after you get settled, you can visit the ranch and see what raising cattle's all about."

"So you're a cattle rancher?"

Tell her who you are! He ignored the voice inside his head. It was too soon for that. He wanted a little more time for her to learn about Chris Wayne. He couldn't tell her his sister Kaytlin ran the ranch while he was gone. "Yes."

"Awesome. How long did you say you're going to be in town?"

"Only for the weekend, why?"

"You'll need to get those stitches out in about 10

days."

He smiled at the thought of what happened in her office yesterday. "Well, maybe I'll just wait 'til you get to San Angelo then I'll come let you take them out." There was that look of concern again. The one he'd seen yesterday when she thought she'd hurt his foot.

"Oh, no! You can't wait that long. They have to come out way before then."

"Don't worry, I'll have my family doctor take them out."

The waiter brought their food and Chris was amazed at how comfortable he was in Shelly's company. He loved to make her laugh and she was radiant when she did. Totally relaxed when they finished their meal, he couldn't bear to see her leave yet. At least not without him.

He put his napkin in his plate and took his last swig of beer. "That was awesome." Shelly seemed relaxed, too, when she met his gaze.

"Agreed. I know I should probably try something else off their menu, but I always order the corn tamale."

"You made a good choice, lady. Have any room left?"

"Maybe, why?"

"I was thinking we could go to an ice cream parlor somewhere and top this meal off with a double dip of something good. Know a good place?"

Shelly was thrilled that Chris seemed to want to

spend more time with her. Now that she knew they were going to live so close to each other, she could see having a relationship with this man. It would still be kind of a long distance one, but at least not as long distance as Vegas and San Angelo. "I know a great place. CJ's Italian Ice & Custard down on Durango."

"Would you like to go?"

"Sure."

Chris pulled out his wallet to pay the bill and she noticed the jeans he had on weren't quite as tight as the ones he'd worn into the office the day before. "I'm proud of you for sticking with a little looser pair of jeans." Although, she would like to see that nice hind-end again, without any jeans at all. His voice drew her from her day-dream.

"Can we take your car?"

She wondered why he'd want to take her vehicle, but, oh well; it didn't matter to her as long as they were together. "Okay with me." He put his cowboy hat on and smiled. She loved the way his gaze warmed when he looked at her. She never thought she'd fall for a cowboy.

"Let's go then." Chris put his hand at the small of Shelly's back and led her to go ahead of him.

The cordiality this man showed was something she hadn't seen in a long while. He seemed to be a straight forward gentleman and she liked that about him. As a matter of fact, so far she liked everything about him. Being with him felt natural, right. She could really like this man.

As they approached her yellow VW Bug, she hoped his tall frame would fit comfortably in the small car. It wasn't new, but she loved it. With all of her student loans to pay off, she was going to wait to get a new car once she was settled in San Angelo.

"Hey, cute car."

"Thanks." Now she almost felt embarrassed by its size, but she watched him take off his hat and slip into the passenger's seat with much grace and no problem at all.

She placed the key in the ignition and started the bug, then heard a cell phone ring. Chris reached into his pocket, slid his finger across the screen and she noticed his hands for the first time. Long slim fingers, well-groomed nails, clean yet strong; how would they feel touching her skin? Hot, she was sure. As hard as she tried, it was impossible not to hear his one-sided conversation.

"Hello."

"Can you give me a couple of hours?"

"Ask the D-man to get it for you."

"No, I don't' want that one."

"Yes, the Gibson and Yamaha."

"Hey, listen, I've gotta go, but I'll be there around four o'clock. That should give us plenty of time."

"Okay, thanks, Madi."

He lowered his voice and almost whispered into the phone, "Love you, too."

Shelly's heart all but stopped. He was talking to a woman named Madi and he loved her. She glanced at him. Married? He wasn't wearing a ring. Engaged? He didn't seem like the type to cheat, but serial killers looked like normal people, too.

CHAPTER 3

Chris hit the end button on his phone, put it back in his pocket and glanced over at Shelly. She had a questioning look in her eyes. "Is something wrong?" He prayed she didn't question what a Gibson and Yamaha were. If he had to tell her they were guitars, she'd have more questions than ever.

"Um...maybe."

"What?" *Oh, hell, here it comes.*

"I couldn't help but overhear you tell someone named Madi you love her."

He realized what must have been going through her mind. He reached and caressed her shoulder. "Madlyn's my little sister. We call her Madi. My older sister's name is Kaytlin." He gave her what he hoped was a reassuring smile. "I'm not married,

Shelly. I don't even have a girlfriend. I wouldn't be here if I did."

She took a deep breath and her frown disappeared. However, he didn't like seeing doubt still in her eyes. "She works with me and needed me to help her make a decision, that's all."

"I'm sorry. I shouldn't have doubted you."

"No problem. I'm glad you asked."

"It's just that, well…I can't stand to be lied to and…" She smiled and met his gaze. "Never mind. I realize you haven't lied to me, so everything's okay."

Now's your chance. Get it out in the open that you're Chris Brock the country singer! His mind shouted to him but he let the thought die to a whisper. He wasn't a liar, but damnit, he didn't want this woman to fall in love with an icon, he wanted her to fall in love with him. He only prayed she'd forgive him when the time came, for not telling her about his career.

Love? That was a strong word. It was one he'd never said to a woman before. At thirty two years old, the only women he had ever told he loved them were his mother and his sisters. Could he be falling in love with Shelly Jinsen?

They pulled into the parking lot of CJ's, but Chris couldn't keep his eyes off of Shelly. She seemed strong yet defenseless, grown up but little girl like. "Shelly?"

She pulled the car to a stop and shut off the engine. "Huh?"

When she turned toward him he fought the urge to pull her into his arms and kiss her. As tempting as it was, this wasn't the place. He wanted to make sure the time was perfect when he tasted her lips. "I'd like to see you again. My time is taken up here in Vegas the rest of the weekend, but maybe when you move to San Angelo we can learn more about each other."

He saw the wheels spinning in her head and he wasn't sure he was going to like what they spun. "Please don't say no. It's been a while since I've said this to a woman, but you're special."

He thought she was special? Shelly swallowed the lump in her throat. More than anything she wanted to discover everything she could about Chris Wayne. "I think that would be nice."

"Awesome. I'll give you my cell number and when you get settled, you can give me a call."

That was something she knew she wouldn't do. "Unfortunately, I don't call guys and ask them out. I have a better idea. Why don't I give you my cell number and you can call me."

He opened the car door stepped out and went around to the driver's side to open her door. "That would be great, but how am I supposed to know when you're settled?"

It had been a long time since a man had opened a door for her and it was nice. She led the way to the ice cream parlor. When he placed his hand in the small of her back and reached around her to open the door to the business, warmth spread through her. His touch comforted her and made the butterflies flitter again.

"Well? How would I know?"

She really didn't want to tell him she'd love to hear from him anytime between now and the time she got semi-established in her new home and job at Shannon Clinic. "Good question." Watching him pay for their treat she added, "You'll just have to guess."

His laugh filled the room and she enjoyed hearing it echo. This man was something else. His tall frame moved with poise across the floor to a table. He once again pulled out her chair and helped her get seated. She could get used to this kind of treatment. She loved the way his eyes smiled when he said her name.

"Shelly, you're leaving yourself open to a call as soon as tomorrow."

Yes! Just what she hoped he'd say. She met his gaze. "I don't think I'd protest."

"That's what I wanted to hear." He shifted in his chair.

"Is your...bu...wound hurting?"

"You started to say my butt didn't you?"

"Yes. That wouldn't be very professional of me though, now would it?"

"You're not a nurse practitioner right now, you're my date. You don't have to be professionally or politically correct when you're with me. Just be yourself. I kind of like it."

Date. It was true, she was actually on a date with this fabulous man. She smiled and winked at him. Now she was flirting! It was crazy but fun. "Your...butt...then. Are you in pain?"

"Would you rub it if I said yes?"

She was enjoying this little game. "Right here? Right now? Umm, I don't think that would be appropriate. Do you?"

"No, I guess not." He liked the little glint in her eye when she answered. Damn he wanted to feel her hands on him again. In a sensual way. Maybe someday. For now, he could only dream.

He enjoyed visiting with the woman on the other side of the table. Their conversation was light hearted, flirtatious and down to earth. Remembering the last time he'd had such a relaxing afternoon with a woman was impossible, because there had never been one.

His cell phone rang. Damn, why wouldn't people allow him time without being disturbed. He couldn't wait to get back to the ranch where he could just be a normal person. Where he could be himself.

Glancing at the caller ID he saw it was Madi again. He swiped his finger across the screen and put the device to his ear. "Hey, Madi, what's up?"

"Where are you? You said you'd be back about four o'clock. They need you for the final sound check. Chris, the show starts in three hours."

He glanced at his watch. Damn, he and Shelly had been talking longer then he thought. "Sorry, sis, I'll be there ASAP."

Worry crossed Shelly's face. "Is something wrong?"

"No, just late for a meeting. I didn't realize we've been talking so long." He put his hand over hers. "I've enjoyed every minute of it, but we'd better go."

Shelly grabbed her purse. "Okay."

They reached the hotel and that voice went off in his head again. *Tell her who you are!* "Shelly…"

She pulled the car under the main entrance awning of Caesars and put it in park. "Yes?"

He just couldn't do it, not yet. "I had a great time." Her smile was genuine and brought a tinge of guilt to his heart. Why couldn't he tell her? What was stopping him? He knew exactly what it was. To this special woman, he wanted to be just plain old Chris Wayne.

"Me, too."

"I'll call you soon." She took a small notebook out of her purse and wrote her number on it. He put it in the shirt pocket next to his heart. The heart this woman had invaded and captured.

"I look forward to it."

Unable to stop himself, he leaned toward her. "May I kiss you?" He was so close to her mouth, her breath was a mere whisper on his lips.

"Yes."

Just as he imagined, she tasted sweet and her lips were soft, warm and made him tingle all over when they gently met his. He heard a deep groan and realized it had come from him. The kiss was easy and pleasurable.

To stop kissing her now was something he didn't want to do, but a slight knock on the car window stole his attention. Shelly looked down and licked her lips. He wondered if he had the same effect on her as she did on him. Another knock, this one louder.

Turning toward the passenger side window, he saw his sister. He grabbed the door handle but before he opened it, he gave Shelly a final, quick goodbye peck on the cheek. "Talk soon."

"K."

He stepped out and shut the car door. Immediately missing Shelly's presence, he watched her drive away. Part of his heart went with her.

Madi took him by the arm. "Come on, everyone's waiting on you." She glanced at the back of the Volkswagen. "Who was that?"

"Her name's Shelly."

"Looks like you were getting pretty cozy."

Not as 'cozy' as he'd like to. His sister was someone he knew he could tell anything to and it would be kept between only them. "She's pretty special. I want to get to know her better."

"Uh-oh. You don't need a groupie in your life, Chris. You know how women are. To her you're probably just a big star she wants to sleep with." She led him through the entrance to the showroom. "Get over it."

He stopped and turned Madi so she'd look him in the eye. "She's different."

"No she's not, Chris. You have never fallen for that, *I like you for you*, crap. Why would you do it now?"

Madi was trying to protect him and he was pleased about that. "She doesn't know."

"Doesn't know what?"

"She doesn't know I'm Chris Brock. She's the nurse practitioner that sewed me up yesterday.

Shelly only knows me as Chris Wayne."

"Seriously? You didn't tell her and she didn't recognize you?"

"Seriously."

"You really like this woman? I mean, really?"

All he could do is nod. Shelly could be his soul mate. He was willing to take a chance on her.

"You're in deep crap then, brother."

"Why do you say that?"

She turned and walked toward the stage. "Because you're trying to start a relationship based on a lie."

He followed. "I didn't lie. I just didn't tell her I'm Chris Brock."

"Same difference, if you ask me."

"Madi, did you hear what you said a few minutes ago about groupies?"

"Sure."

"That's why I didn't tell her. I don't want her to be like the others."

"Sounds like you don't have very much confidence in her as a person. If you think she's that shallow, and would act like all the others, then maybe she's not the woman you think she is."

Damnit! Now he realized he should have told her. He made a decision at that moment. "You're right. Monday I'll go by her office and come clean. It will either happen between us or it won't."

"Why don't you call her. The sooner the better?"

He thought about her cell number in his pocket. "I want to tell her face to face."

"You'll be lucky if she doesn't kick your ass out."

"Thanks for the reassurance." He heard the D-man's voice ring in the large empty room that, in just a few hours, would be full of fans for the Friday night show.

"It's about time!"

Chris walked over to his new $4,500 Gibson guitar. He'd never spent that much money on a guitar before, but he was glad to accept it from Gibson as a gift because he endorsed their company. He picked it up, put the strap around his shoulder then strummed the strings. Perfectly tuned. He loved Gibson.

He placed his ear monitors in then put his microphone headset in place. It was awesome not having to stand in front of a mic stand. Even his guitar was hooked to his amp wirelessly. It allowed him to cover the stage completely.

"Where the hell have you been, Chris? We've been waiting for over fifteen minutes. You're never late."

"You remember that nurse that sewed me up yesterday?"

"The doctor nurse?"

"Doctor nurse?" He laughed. "Yes, that one."

"Yeah, I remember her. Why?"

"We went to lunch today then out for ice cream. I let time get away from me, that's all."

"Did you get lucky?"

Chris shook his head. Why did musicians think if you went out with a woman you had to bed them to prove your manhood or something? "No, I like her. I really like her. Maybe even love her."

"In all the years I've known you, that's the first

time I've heard you say you really like someone. But love? Chris, come on. There's no such thing as love at first sight or love on first date."

Right now, Chris wasn't so sure about that. He missed her at that very moment. "Maybe not, but she's different." A deep voice from nowhere sounded in his ear monitor and he knew it was the sound man in the booth.

"You ready to get started, Mr. Brock?"

He spoke into his headset. "Ready." The rest of the band finished their last minute tuning then Chris turned to the drummer. "Count off Heaven."

Clicking his drumsticks to the tempo the man said, "One, two, three, four."

Chris strummed a G chord and began to sing, "Heaven is my woman's love..." His thoughts drifted to Shelly. Could she be the one?

CHAPTER 4

Shelly was getting excited about going to the Chris Brock concert. It had been a while since she'd been to a show like his and she looked forward to it. Heck, it had been a while since she'd been out on a Saturday night.

Knowing she didn't have any real western wear, she searched her closet for the perfect outfit. To her delight, she found an old pair of faded jeans that, with the holes in them, were in style. She chose a white tank top and decided this was a great opportunity to wear the turquoise squash blossom neckless, matching bracelet and ring her sister Sarah gave her when she graduated NP school.

She took the new pair of cowboy boots she bought out of the box. It was the first she'd ever owned and she hoped by the end of the evening her feet weren't killing her. Once she pulled them on and tucked her jean legs into them, she realized they were very comfortable. The belt she purchased fit great and the western buckle reminded her of the one on Chris Wayne's belt. She still wondered why it had CB on it instead of CW, but it was no big deal.

With one last glance in her full length mirror, she was surprised that she looked like...a cowgirl. A small bit of her belly showed, but that was supposed to be stylish. She had pulled part of her hair up into a messy bun like her hairdresser JP, queen of the messy bun, had showed her. It wasn't as good as JP would have done it, but it was okay. Some long tendrils still hung over her shoulders.

After coloring it that afternoon, she decided she liked it. The darker color was rich and shiny. She fluffed the top then the doorbell rang. Glancing down at her Yorkie puppy she said, "That's Sid, Harley. Time to go in your kennel."

The cute little fur ball did as instructed, and Shelly gave her a treat. "Be a good girl. I'll be home in a little while." She shut the wire cage gate, took what she thought she would need out of her purse and stuck it in her back pocket. Carrying a bag was too much of a responsibility for a concert. She wanted to let loose and have fun. She grabbed her cell phone from the table as she walked by and stuck it into her other back pocket. It was a tight fit, but she didn't want to leave it behind.

Opening the door, she was greeted by Sidne and...Josh? "Well, this is a surprise. I didn't know you were the one going with us, Josh."

"Yes, ma'am. I'll be the designated driver for you ladies tonight."

"Wow!" Sidne grabbed her by the shoulders and turned her around. "You look great! I thought you didn't care too much for country music. You make a beautiful cowgirl!"

Josh whistled out loud. "I second that!"

Heat rose to her face and neck. "Stop, you're making me blush." She wished Chris could see her now. Maybe he'd think the same thing. However, that was impossible. She hadn't heard from him since their lunch date the day before, but she figured he was busy buying cattle.

"We'd better go ladies. I'm sure the line will be long, even though we already have our tickets."

Josh had been right. The line was long, but it moved quickly. She was pleased they got through so fast. "Boy, you weren't kidding when you said we are front and center were you, Sid."

"Nope. My aunt Sharon works in the ticket office. She told me Chris was coming and I could have her discount, which is huge, I told her to get me three of the best."

"I love your aunt Sharon!" Their seats weren't more than ten feet from the stage. There were steps all the way around it. "I wonder if the musicians ever come out into the audience."

"Aunt Sharon said one time Celine Dion came off stage and kissed my uncle right on his bald head! So, I guess they can if they want to."

The crowd filtered in and the echo of the large room became full of chatter, laughter and excitement. Once the lights came down, the audience got quiet. She found herself anticipating the opening of the curtains.

Touching Sid on the hand she leaned closer to her. "Thank you for inviting me." Sidne nodded then the music started and the curtain opened. The musicians were all dressed in cowboy attire and a man, she assumed was Chris Brock, stood with his back to the audience holding a white guitar.

A voice came from the surround sound PA system. "And now ladies and gentleman, Caesars Palace presents, Chris Brock!"

The audience went wild and the tall singer turned around. His cowboy hat shaded his face when he started to sing. Shelly's heart pumped wild as she got caught up in the enthusiasm.

"I got me a room, in a cheap hotel. My head was a spinnin' and I didn't feel well…"

Shelly began to feel the grove to the music and she watched Chris Brock as he mastered the song. "Man, he's good!"

Sidne clapped her hands to the rhythm. "Told ya!"

Then she glanced at the big screen on the side of the stage and thought her heart, that was beating wildly a minute ago, would stop completely. "Chris!" She saw the singers face clearly for the first time. It was Chris Wayne! CB! The buckle! No wonder it had CB on it. He was Chris Brock!

That no good lying rat! Why hadn't he told her who he really was? If there's one thing she couldn't tolerate, it was a liar. The man she thought was a, good ole cattle ranching country boy, was…a big ole country music star!

She swallowed the bile in her throat. Her hopes of having a relationship with Chris Wayne flew out the window. He hadn't thought enough of her to want her to know he was Chris Brock. Lies. How much of what he told her had been lies?

Tears welled in her eyes, but she blinked them back. She grabbed Sidne by the arm and saw the uneasiness in the younger woman's gaze.

"What's wrong, Shel?"

Pointing at the stage she replied, "It's Chris!"

"I know!"

Panic struck and she began to tremble. "You know?"

"Chris Brock. Sure, I know."

"No, Sidne, that's Chris Wayne. The cowboy with the glass in his ass." A look of shear surprise captured the younger woman's face. Shelly nodded toward the big screen where his face was clear. "Look!"

"OMG! It *is* him. I can't believe I didn't recognize him yesterday."

"Probably because you were looking at his butt, not his face." She turned to go. "I've got to get out of here." She needed to leave before he saw and recognized her. Creating a scene was out of the question. Sid gently grabbed her arm and she twisted to meet her gaze.

"Come on, Shelly, the concert just started."

"I don't want him to see me."

"Why not?"

"I have my reasons."

"Please, Shel? Just think, with the stage lights in his eyes, he probably can't see us anyway."

Sidne's pleading look melted her heart. How could she be so selfish. She couldn't force her friends to leave just because she didn't want to deal with Chris...whatever his name was. "Okay. I'll stay, but at intermission I'm going to call a cab and go home."

"Fair enough."

The man she knew as Chris Wayne danced on stage while his band played a lead ride. His jeans were tight and fit to a tee. *I hope those tight jeans are killing your ass!* Damn he was one hunk of a man. How could she continue to be attracted to a liar?

Throughout the first part of the show she tried to stay calm and not bring attention to herself. The more she listened to the music, the more she became engulfed in the party atmosphere. Chris was definitely the leader of his band and she could tell his musicians adored him.

Nice guy or not, they couldn't have a relationship based on a li– "Oh, no!" When Chris turned his back to the audience she saw a small dark spot on his pants, right where his sutures were. *He's bleeding!* She chastised herself for wishing his butt was hurting. It probably really was. "Damn."

How was she going to get his attention? She didn't want to get his attention. That's what she had been avoiding all evening, but she couldn't let him bleed out on his jeans in front of all of these people!

Everyone in the colosseum was standing including her. She stepped forward and got closer to the stage when she felt Sidne grab her arm.

"What are you doing?"

"I have to get Chris' attention."

"Why, I thought you didn't want him to know you're here?"

"His butt is bleeding through his jeans. I think he broke his stitches open."

"Oh, crap!"

"I know. Right?" She watched Chris as he approached the edge of the stage close to her then she waved at him. Nothing. Maybe he was so engrossed in his performance he wasn't paying attention to the audience.

She waved again and he met her gaze. The eye contact threatened to take her breath, and the moment he recognized her a strange expression crossed his face. Was that fear? Disappointment? It was apparent he didn't think he'd see her there.

Mouthing her words, she pointed at herself then to him. "I need to talk to you." Then he smiled as if he was actually glad to see her. His face lit up and those damned butterflies started to quiver. This was ridiculous. He had lied to her yet he still caused this effect. She mouthed the words again, hoping he would get the gist of what she was trying to say.

Then she pointed to her rear hoping he would understand. "You're bleeding."

Now he was totally focused on her, but she knew he had no idea what she was trying to say. The song was over and the crowd roared. Chris stepped right in front of her, then took a step down the stairs toward her. His voice was loud and clear over the audio system.

"Thank you, thank you so much! I'd like to invite a friend of mine to join me on stage."

No, he wasn't going to ask her up there...was he? He held his hand out toward her. "Come on up here, Shelly."

She shook her head. "No way." He couldn't hear her, but surely he wasn't crazy enough to think she was going up on the main stage of the Caesars Palace Colosseum. She could speak in front of her classmates at college, but to stand in front of hundreds of people while in the spotlight? That was another question. No matter if she said anything or not.

"Folks, let's give the lady a big round of applause so she'll join me up here. What do you say?"

Now she was the one defeated. Somehow she had to tell him his back side was bleeding. Soon the blood stain would be big enough for everyone to see if he turned his back on the auditorium. *Put on your big girl panties and get up there. He has to know what's going on.*

She didn't know what she was worried about. Speaking in front of people was nothing new to her. This, however, was different than speaking in front of fifty or a hundred people, she knew that, but if getting on stage meant she would get through to him then she guessed she'd have to do just that.

*Note to self. I am going to **kill** him when this is over. Chris Way...Brock...you are one dead cowboy.*

Chris couldn't believe his eyes when he saw Shelly Jinsen making her way up the stage steps.

Man, did she look hot! She made the most beautiful, sexy cowgirl he'd ever seen.

He never would have expected to see her here. Especially waving at him like a...grou...no, he refused to think she wanted to be a groupie. The other girls that clambered at the stage and tried to grab him every chance they got were smiling and attempting to look sexy. Shelly, on the other hand, looked pissed, sexy and determined she was going to tell him something whether he wanted to hear it or not.

Oh, crap! Now she knows the truth and probably wants to tell me to go to hell! He feared it would ruin any chance of her getting a better insight of him as normal person and not as Chris Brock.

The applause was tremendous when she took the top step. He leaned towards the most gorgeous woman in the world and held his hand out to her. Only he could tell her smile was fake, but he was fascinated she put on such a good show.

He motioned for a stage hand to bring out a corded mic. The man rushed to get the device in the middle of the stage. Chris walked her to the center of the stage and stepped up to the microphone. "Ladies and gentleman, I'd like to introduce Doc. Shelly!" Clapping hands and yeehaws reverberated throughout the building.

When he met her gaze he saw...concern in her eyes? What was going on? He didn't know, but the show had to go on. "I'm going to sing this next one for you, Doc. It's called, *Heaven is My Woman's Love*. It's my newest #1 hit." He glanced out at the crowd. "Anyone heard this song before?" He was proud of his version of the Tommy Overstreet hit from years ago. "Great, then you can join in and sing along."

Dropping Shelly's hand, he turned to reach for his guitar, but she stopped him. It was a total surprise when she picked up the instrument and handed it to him. "Why, thank ya, Doc." He saw her lips moving but couldn't hear her over the roar of the crowd.

Oh, my gosh! How was she going to tell him about his bleed if he couldn't hear her? It was too late, the band kicked off the song and Chris began to sing.

"Heaven is my woman's love...and gently rising with the sun...she gives me cause to face the day...and gives me joy when day is done..."

He looked at her on that line and raised his eyebrows up and down. How dare he allude to all these people that she may have brought him 'joy' at the end of his day. If she was more of a sadist, she'd poke the sore spot on his backside! Oaf! No, lying oaf! Lying to her *and* the audience!

Was she crazy? The more she listened to the words of the song, and saw the way he looked at her, the more she started to relax and enjoyed him singing to her.

"And when I see her in the morning light...I feel the same as in the dark of night...She is my everything and I'm proud of...the heaven of my woman's love...

"Heaven is my woman's love...gently reaching

out for me…all she wants is what I am…searching not for what I'll be…"

When she met his gaze through the lines of that verse, there was pleading in his eyes. His words now were in the background as she remembered what he'd just sang…all she wants is what I am…searching not for what I'll be…. Why did those words hit her so strongly?

As the song ended, she brought herself out of the trance he'd put her in while looking into his beautiful eyes and lulled by his awesome voice along with the words of the song. She had to tell him about his butt bleeding.

He put his arm around her waist and kissed her on the forehead. What? The audience went wild when she looked up at him, met his gaze and he bent and gently kissed her lips. In front of the whole of Vegas? Was *he* crazy? She had to admit she enjoyed it, but she couldn't forget the lies that had come from the very lips that had just made her feel warm and fuzzy.

She kept the smile on her face and said, "Your ass is bleeding." Her heart all but stopped when she heard his voice on the microphone.

"Wait, folks, the doc want's to say something."

She shook her head. "No, no. Not on the microphone."

"Say what, Doc?"

He shoved the mic in her face. What was she going to do? "Um, ummm, thanks for the song, Chris." She glanced out at the standing people. "What do y'all think about Chris Brock? Isn't he awesome?!" The applause was deafening. Now it was time to ding his ear. Literally.

She tried to yell out of the corner of her mouth so no one would see. "Your butt's bleeding." He shook his head and she knew he didn't hear.

In a louder tone she tried to yell above the noise of the crowd, to no avail. She had to take drastic action. Reaching up, she grabbed Chris by the earlobe and pulled him down so he could hear her. Even more cheers from the audience. Did they think she was blowing in his ear? Whatever!

"Chris, your stiches broke loose and your *ass* is bleeding! The back of your jeans are getting stained with blood. Don't turn your back to your, *hoard* of fans, or they'll see it."

Was that sarcasm he heard in her voice? He continued to smile down at her and listened to the people chant. 'Chris, Chris, Chris…' "What do you suggest, Doc?"

"How long before intermission?"

"About 15 minutes."

"My office isn't far. I'll go get what I need to fix you up and be back by the time you take a break."

She was so beautiful he wanted to take her in his arms and give her a full blown kiss right here in front of God and everybody. However, the look in her eyes said she'd slap the hell out of him if he tried to kiss her again.

He turned toward the people. "Y'all give a big round of gratitude to the Shelly for coming up here."

She smiled up at him. "I told you not to wear

tight jeans."

Abruptly she turned and headed toward the stairs that led off the stage. He watched her smile and wave at the crowd. Impressed by her ability to act like she was happy, when he knew she was fuming, his admiration for her grew.

Guitar in hand, he strummed a chord and started the next song. His heart leapt at the thought of seeing her again in a few minutes, although he wasn't looking forward to her having a sharp object close to his wound. Not in the mood she was in.

CHAPTER 5

That big lug of a cowboy was on her list. She couldn't wait to tell him what she thought of him, but for now, she had to do her job.

She approached Sidne and Josh, her throat hurt when she tried to make them hear her over the music. "I have to go to the office and grab some stuff to stich him up." Sidne had a silly grin on her face.

"You looked great up there. I think that man really likes you."

She didn't want to talk about that now; she had more pressing things at hand. Whether he liked her or not, it didn't matter now. She'd made up her mind it would never work. She refused to fall in love with a liar. "Sid, it was all put on. Pretend, make-believe...you know, put on a show. All I went up there for was to tell him he needed medical care."

"Oh, really? That kiss didn't look too fake."

Remembering how she felt when he sang to her, and when he'd kissed her, made her desire for him kick in to high gear. She could fall in lov...NO! She looked at Josh. "Give me your keys. I don't want y'all to miss the rest of the first half."

Josh reached into his pocket. "You sure you don't want me to take you?"

"I'll be fine." She took the car keys from him. "I'll be back in time to sew him up during intermission." Sidne touched her arm and got her attention.

"Hey, if you need some help holler at me. I wouldn't mind seeing that nice, round tush of his again."

A surge of jealousy shot through her. She didn't want any woman besides herself seeing his nice, round tush.

Where did that come from? She knew, but pushed the feeling deep down inside her. It was ridiculous. "Okay, Sid, I'll yell if I need you."

She glanced at her watch. Only ten minutes 'til the break. She had to hurry. Making her way against the crowd, she felt like a fish swimming upstream in a downstream currant, but finally she made her way to the lobby.

Finding the car was another thing. Where the heck had Josh parked. She didn't have time for nonsense; she had to get on the road. The only thing she could think to do was push the panic button. Surely the horn honking would help her find the vehicle.

"Here goes." The red button gave beneath her finger and sure enough a horn began to honk. She scanned the lot and saw the flashing lights of Josh's car then walked toward it.

Inside she started the engine, shut the door and headed to the clinic wondering how she was going to feel when she was alone with Chris suturing his butt. Now wasn't the time to think about her emotions.

Once she arrived the parking lot was lit, but the building was dark. She went to the back door of the clinic, unlocked it then went inside. Only a couple of minutes left. Flipping on the hall light, she hurried to the supply room, gathered the things she needed and…Wait…her heart hammered. What was that noise? Had someone followed her? Was someone in the building with her?

She swallowed and tried to force down the bile that rose in her throat. What should she do? *Call the police, stupid.* She pulled out her cell phone and dialed.

"911, what is your emergency?"

She heard a woman's voice from the hallway. What the hell was going on?

"Doc. Shelly? Are you here?"

Her mind was reeling. Who could that be?

"911, what is your emergency?"

She whispered into the phone. "I'm not sure. This is Shelly Jinsen. I'm a nurse practitioner at the Health and Wellness Clinic. I had to–"

"Doc. Shelly? I'm Madi, Chris' sister. Are you here?"

Chris' sister? Why in the world would she be at the clinic? She turned her attention back to the 911 operator. "I don't think there is an emergency, but could you stay with me for a moment while I make sure?"

"Ma'am, don't put yourself in danger. I'll send a patrol unit out right away."

Shelly stepped out of the supply room and saw a beautiful redhead standing in the hallway. She had the same blue eyes as her brother. There was no mistaking she was Chris Way...Brock's sister.

She lifted her phone to her ear. "Ma'am? There is no emergency. No need to send a patrol car."

"Is someone making you say that, Ms. Jinsen?"

A chuckle escaped her. "No, not at all. I'm fine. Thank you."

"Yes, ma'am, have a blessed evening."

Hitting the end call button, she studied the lady in front of her. "Madi, Chris told me about you, but why are you here?" The woman smiled showing straight, white teeth and lots of personality flowed from her gaze.

"All I can say, is my brother must really like you. He noticed you left the colosseum alone and was worried something might happen to you. He sent me..." She patted her side. "And my trusty persuader, to make sure you got back to him safely."

"You mean, you carry a gun?" She couldn't believe this petite little thing was a pistol packin' mama."

"I sure do. Would you like to see it? We live on a ranch, and being with a big country star like Chris, you have to be prepared for anything that comes your way."

"No, I don't need to see it. I believe you." She looked at her watch and her concern grew. "We have to hurry. It'll be time for him to go back on to finish the show by the time we get back."

"You're right." Madi turned and headed toward the door.

"Wait, I have an idea." She went into the supply room again, grabbed some gauze and waterproof tape then joined Madi in the hallway. "I'll just bandage him up then I can re-suture him after the show."

"That's a great idea. It will save time for sure."

She turned off the lights, followed the red haired woman outside then locked the door. Madi touched her arm gently.

"Doc. Shelly?"

"Please, I'm not a doctor, just call me Shelly."

"Okay." Madi dropped her hand. "I really appreciate what you've done for Chris. You're a special lady and he knows it."

After she opened the door of Josh's car she placed her bag inside. "Yeah, well…" If he really thought she was so special, he wouldn't have lied to her. She told him she couldn't stand a liar, and he'd done it anyway.

The woman reached the spot where her SUV was. "Follow me. We'll park at the back stage door and go in that way. It's more private and a lot closer, too."

"Sounds good." She got in the car and all the way to Caesars all she could think about was if

Chris thought she was so special, why did he lie to her? Why couldn't he just be honest?

The words he sang to her with such sincerity in his eyes ran through her mind. "Heaven is my woman's love...gently reaching out for me...all she wants is what I am...searching not for what I'll be..."

"All she wants is what I am. Searching not for what I'll be." That's it! He didn't want her to know he was a country music singer. But why? Now she was even more confused.

Madi's break lights went on as she pulled to a stop at the back entrance of the colosseum then got out of the SUV. Shelly pulled in behind her, grabbed her bag and got out of the car. "Which way?"

"Come on, I'll show you."

It was darker behind the stage than she had expected. Even though she'd been outside in the dark, this dimness was different but her eyes finally adjusted. They made their way over cords, through pipe and draped walkways then into a well-lit hallway.

Stopping at a door with a big yellow star on it, Madi knocked. "We're here?"

In seconds the door flew open and there he was in all of his handsomeness. *Breathe, Shelly, breathe.* She forced air into her lungs and swished past him. Music started in the main arena and the crowd came alive. "Let's get this over with."

Chris unbuckled his belt, unzipped his pants and

leaned over the desk with his backside exposed. It wasn't anything Shelly hadn't seen before, but he wasn't that comfortable with Madi being in the room to witness him getting his butt sewn up. "Are you going to have time to stich me up?"

"I'm not going to suture you right now. I'm going to put on a bandage that will prevent the blood from staining your pants any more. We'll sew you up when the show's over."

He winced when she rubbed a cold substance on the wound. "Damn, could you be a little gentler? That's sore you know."

"Mr. Wayne, or Brock, or whoever you are. If you'd done what I advised and not worn such tight jeans, you wouldn't be in this situation right now. I suggest you shut up and let me do my job, so you can get back to yours."

"Look, Shelly, I'm sorry I didn't tell you who–" Another stab of pain while she pressed on the cut, he assumed, to make it stop bleeding.

"Didn't tell me who you are? Is that what you were going to say?"

"Yes, but–"

"Lied is more like it. You not only didn't tell me what you really do for a living, you lied and said you are a cattle rancher."

The warmth of her hand putting the gauze in place was a much welcome difference than the cold liquid she applied only seconds before. "I *am* a cattle rancher." Madi's voice drew his attention.

"Oooh, I told you."

Shelly tore some tape from the roll and glanced at Madi. "Told him what?"

"Sis, stay out of this, will you? It's between me and Shelly." Two sharp slaps hit his backside when Shelly applied the first piece of tape then the second.

"At this point, we are only NP and patient. There is *nothing* between you and me, Mr. Wayne. Nothing." She turned toward her bag and placed the supplies inside. "Now you'd better go appease your followers." She once again faced him. "Do I make myself clear?"

How in the hell was he ever going to make this better? He thought he was falling in love with the woman in front of him, but he'd ruined it! "Shelly, plea–"

She held up her hand. "No...go...your fans are calling your name."

The last thing he wanted to do was leave her feeling like this, but she was right. The show must go on.

Shelly almost went limp when Chris left the room. She had to sit down and found the first chair she came to. Tears threatened to spill onto her cheek. Why was this happening? She could love him so easily. Why did he have to be a liar?

She had all but forgotten Madi was still in the room. The sound of the woman walking toward her, made her straighten and try to smile. It was no use, she was too sad.

"Shelly?"

"Madi, I'm so sorry you had to hear all of that." She felt the slight squeeze Madi gave her hand.

"No worries." She sat in a chair opposite Shelly. "I want to tell you something, but only if you want me to. I'm really not one to interfere, but I think there's something you should know."

She met the woman's sincere gaze. "Do I really want to know?"

Smiling, Madi said, "I think so."

A tear slipped onto her cheek. It was useless to try to blink them back. Madi's kindness was more then she could bear yet she feared what she was about to hear. "Go ahead." She reached into her bag and got a piece of gauze to wipe her tears with. She felt a gusher coming on.

"Chris is anything *but* a liar."

"How can you stick up for him?" That was a stupid question. She was his sister. Of course she was going to take his side. "Never mind." Now she was being rude, and all Madi wanted to do was help. "I'm sorry, Madi, go on."

"I know you're frustrated right now, and you have every right to be, but please hear me out."

She wiped her face again and met Madi's gaze. "I'm listening."

Madi sat back and started to talk, "I saw Chris get out of your VW in the parking lot. I figured you were just another groupie and warned him about you.

"You see, women flock around him like flies. They want to 'sleep with a star', you might say. But my brother doesn't go for that kind of stuff like a lot of musicians do.

"He said you weren't like the rest, but I thought he was falling for some line you gave him. That's when he told me you didn't know he was Chris Brock. You only knew him as Chris Wayne."

This was getting more interesting every minute. "Soooo…"

Madi stood, went to a fridge and got two bottles of water. She handed one to Shelly, opened hers, took a sip then sat back down. "So, I told him the truth."

"And what's that."

"That he was probably in deep crap. He couldn't understand why, so I told him he was trying to start a relationship based on a lie."

Shelly took a drink of water. Madi was a smart woman. "Exactly!"

"Girl, you know as well as I do, men don't think like us. He didn't think he lied, he just thought it was okay he didn't tell you he is Chris Brock."

"But why?" Shelly shook her head. "I don't understand."

"Hey." She reached over and touched Shelly's leg. "He really likes you. He wanted you to know him as himself before you knew he is a star.

"Once I told him he'd done the wrong thing, he immediately knew he'd made a mistake and on Monday was going to come into your office and tell you everything. However, now the situation stands as it is."

Every emotion Shelly had was on her sleeve. She was excited to know his feelings were real, but she was sad to know he didn't have the confidence in her to be honest. Yet, she saw his point and was sympathetic to his dilemma.

Was she really sympathetic, or was she making

an excuse to forgive him and try again. She was so confused. "Madi, I don't know what to do." She looked into the woman's blue eyes that reminded her of Chris'. She liked the redhead already.

Standing, Madi said, "Um, I'd go with my heart if I were you. I mean, Chris is a good man and I've never seen him interested in a woman the way he is in you. Just sayin'...

"Now, I'm going to leave you to your thoughts. I'll keep your friends entertained after the concert 'til you get through dealing with that *ass* of a brother of mine. Oh, no pun intended." Laughing, Madi went out of the room and closed the door.

~~~~

Chris did one encore and could have done a second, but he was too anxious to get back to Shelly and see if he could make things right between them. Why the hell he hadn't been smart enough to be honest with her, he didn't know.

Not knowing what to expect, he turned the knob on his dressing room door. Shelly stood by the desk, arms folded. He couldn't read the look on her face. Glancing down, all of her suture equipment lay on the desktop. It had been totally cleaned off and covered with sterile paper.

Shelly uncrossed her arms. "Come on in, *Mr. Brock!*"

This was *not* going to be good. The way she held out his name said it all. She was still pissed. He figured the best way to handle this was to do whatever she said. "Yes, ma'am."

"Are you ready?" She picked up a syringe, inspected it then laid it back on the clean white disposable cloth. "You know I'm going to have to take the stitches out that are still in place, deaden and clean the area then re-suture it, right?"

Was he ready to do this in his dressing room? Alone with a NP who was mad at him? "Maybe we should get your friend and go to your office to do this." Her smile was wickedly beautiful and it turned him on, although he was a bit frightened at the same time.

She shook her head. "Not. A. Chance. Now get those boots and pants off." She walked to the closet. "I see you were smart enough to keep some sweats on hand. You can put these on after we finish up here."

"No, really, do you want to go to the off–"

"Uh, uh. We are going to stay right here until we get everything done we need to get done."

Chris took off his boots, socks and pants then stood in his boxers and shirt looking sexy as hell. If he knew what was in store for him, he'd probably run. "You're such a good boy. Now, drop those shorts and expose your cheek." She was having too much fun playing with his psyche.

Maybe she *was* being a little too hard on him. "No, really, just relax. This will be over soon."

"Over?" He turned to face her. "That's what I'm afraid of." He stepped toward her. "I don't want it…us…to be over."

It was all she could do not to leap into his arms and tell him it was anything but over. However, she had to make him understand she refused to be lied to, no matter what intentions were behind the dishonesties.

"Let's get you sewn up, dressed, then we can talk."

He smiled. "So you're willing to talk about it?"

"Chris! Bend your ass over that table. Now!" She was surprised how fast he followed her orders and she smiled at his vulnerability. "Drop your drawers! Relax that cheek by putting your weight on the other leg. This won't take long."

"Damn, you don't have to be so bossy." He pulled his shorts down enough to expose the area.

"And you don't have to cuss."

"Oh, so *ass* isn't a cuss word?"

"No, *ass* is the name of an animal." She ripped the tape and gauze from his skin.

"Ouch, do you have to be so rough?"

Without answering, she continued her speech, "Being a ranch owner I'd think you'd know the term jackass is used to signify a male donkey. A donkey is a domesticated *ass*." She stuck the numbing needle deep into the wound.

"Ouch!"

"Oh, stop whining." She finished putting the medicine in then popped the plastic cover over the needle and disposed of it. "The *ass* is a species related to the horse and part of the equidae family. That family is related to the equines but is found wild in Africa and Asia. Zebra are in that family, too. But! No pun intended, the male ass is called "a jack," thus the term jackass."

Wow, good job! If she could pat herself on the

back she would. She had looked the term up on her phone hoping she could use the word during this very conversation. She was proud and laughed in her mind. It worked out perfectly.

"Good Lord, did you do research on that? You sound like a dictionary."

"Nope, I'm just smart that way." She refused to tell him the truth. Poking at the cut on his butt cheek she asked, "Can you feel that?"

"Feel what?"

"Good, I'd say we're ready to put the stitches in." She guessed she'd have to tell him the truth. Her little white lie put her in the same category as him. It would be impossible to get on to him for not being honest, if she did the same thing.

"Great, let's get this over with."

"Okay," She grabbed what she needed and started to suture. "And truthfully, I did look the word ass up on my phone."

"Awww, did you do that just for me?"

"Don't be smart. I have a sharp object in my hand." He rested his head on his hands and she knew he tried to relax as much as he could.

"Shelly?"

"Yes."

"What I said earlier, about it…us…being over?"

"Yes."

"I mean it. I don't want it to be over. I'm sorry I lied to you. I didn't really think I was lying, I just thought I wasn't telling you. Madi set me straight on that. Really, I was planning to come to your office Monday to tell you everything."

She could hardly hold down her happiness. He

really *did* care for her. He was telling the truth, too, Madi confirmed that, but did she dare trust him? Her heart said yes, but her mind said 'danger'. Like Madi said, she had to go with her heart. It was all but impossible to stay angry at him when she'd already made her decision. Yet she didn't speak.

"Shelly? Did you hear me?"

She tied the last stitch. The pleading in his voice stole her heart but she tried to keep up her angry act. "Of course I heard you. We're the only two in the room.

"So you believe me?"

"Yes. But, Chris Brock Wayne, you listen to me and you listen good! I–" He started talking before she could finish what she had to say.

"I'll listen, I promise, but can we wait 'til you get done fixing my butt so I can be in a little less…compromising…position   while   I'm listening?"

It was all she could do to keep from laughing. Poor guy, he was in an awfully vulnerable spot. "I'll snip the last suture now." She tossed the used curved suture needle and the needle driver onto the table, picked up the sterile scissors and cut the string then tossed them onto the table, too. "As soon as I put a fresh bandage on, you can put your clothes on."

He was quiet while she covered the wound. Happiness flowed through her at what the outcome of this conversation might bring. She pulled her gloves off with a snap, threw them on the table then patted him on the round part of his bottom. "Okay, you can get dressed now, cowboy."

EPILOGUE

As they slipped into their bed, Shelly thought of the changes in her and Chris' lives over the last eighteen or so months. "I'm so glad I decided to move to the ranch. I miss my job at the clinic, but taking care of the hands' injuries is almost a full time job. Plus being on the road with you, I wouldn't have time to work.

"I love you, Mrs. Wayne."

Shelly gazed at the man lying next to her. "I love you, too, Mr. Wayne." The smile in his eyes made her warm all over. It had been over a year since their wedding and she loved him more today than she did then.

"You know what today is, don't you?"

"Nothing special that I know of."

"Well, it's–"

The dog scratched at Chris' side of the bed and she watched her husband turn over and reach for the little pooch. She racked her brain to try to figure out what he was talking about being special, but his bare backside was visible from beneath the covers and she couldn't think of anything else. "I see your butt."

He put the dog on the covers between them. "See I knew you'd remember."

"Harley, stop licking my face. I love you, too. You don't have to be jealous." The Yorkie went to the foot of the bed, turned in a couple of circles then laid down in a curled up ball of fluff. She turned her attention back to her husband. "I have no idea what you're talking about, honey."

The fake, pouting look on his face didn't fool her. She knew she really hadn't hurt his feelings. "Stop playing around. What was so special about today?"

"My butt."

"What? I love your butt. However, it's no more special today than it was yesterday." She placed her hand on his head to see if he had a fever. "Are you feeling okay?"

His laughter rang through the air and he scooched closer to her then took her in his arms. "I feel great!"

"Then what's wrong with you?" She settled into his embrace, loving the warmth and safety she felt.

"Today was, is our second anniversary."

"No it's not. We've only been married a year."

He took her hand and slid it down so it rested on his bottom. "I know that. This is the second anniversary of the first time you touched my…derriere."

She gave his backside a sharp slap then began to rub where she smacked him. It made her feel good that he remembered when she didn't. "Chris Wayne, you mean you know the exact date I sewed you up?" He kissed her gently then cupped one of her breasts with his hand. She loved this man more than life itself. When he ended the kiss, she missed the taste of him.

"I sure do." He kissed her again. "It's the day I met the most beautiful woman in the world. The love of my life. My soul mate. My wife."

After all the times she and Chris had made love, butterflies deep in her stomach should have stopped dancing, but on occasion, they still fluttered sending a rush of excitement through her. This man made her want him so much. She could never have imagined love being so wonderful.

He reached up and turned off the bedside light. The darkness of night would hold passion, but they were one soul in the light of love.

ABOUT THE AUTHOR

Sharon Kizziah-Holmes

I live in the beautiful Ozarks with my husband our Cocker Spaniel Dude, and Waylon our hound dog. I have seventeen grandkids and seven great grands and one on the way. I love each and every one of them with all my heart and can't wait for the new arrival.

My interest in writing novels came in the early 1990's. A friend suggested we write a book together, so I took her up on it. I joined writing groups and a whole new world opened up for me. I'm still a member of many writing groups. I absolutely love writing, editing, publishing and teaching the basics of writing to others.

Over the years I've written a story for all but one of my niece's and their spouses, and one for my nephew and his spouse. Shelly and Chris' story is last to make it to paper, but it means as much as to me as the other stories do.

I'm so happy these two found each other and have such a strong love between them, as do all four of these happily married couples. Through them, I have great nieces and a great, great niece and nephew.

My life is blessed.